Say Hello to the Animals!

Ian Whybrow   Tim Warnes

Sandy Creek
NEW YORK

Ready, steady, off we go.
Round the farm to say hello.

Who's that nibbling, half asleep?
Say hello to the dozy sheep.

Hello, Sheep!
Baaa, baaa, baaa!

Here's the sty – not very big –
Say hello to the little pink pig.

Hello, Pig!
Oink, oink, oink!

Who's on the fence beside her pen?
Say hello to the speckly hen.

Look who's hiding under those sticks.
Say hello to the fluffy chicks.

Hello, Chicks!
Cheep, cheep, cheep!

Look in the barn – who's in here now?
Say hello to the friendly cow.

Hello, Cow!

Moo, moo, moo!

Who's that paddling in the muck?
Say hello to the splashy duck.

Who's in the stable? Yes, of course!
Say hello to the hungry horse.

Hello, Horse!

Neigh, neigh, neigh!

What a lot of animals, my, oh my!
Now it's time to say goodbye.

Goodbye, Cow!
MOO, mOO, mOO!

Goodbye, Hen!
Cluck, cluck, cluck!

Goodbye, Pigs!
Oink, oink, oink!

Goodbye, Chicks!
Cheep, cheep, cheep!

"Are you ready, Ella Rose? Off you go with your Hellos!"
With a Hello and a big whiskery kiss from You-know-who. – I.W.

For Nick, Anna, Fraser and Alex:
"Hello you Lows!" –T.W.

Sandy Creek
NEW YORK

An Imprint of Sterling Publishing
1166 Avenue of the Americas
New York, NY 10036

SANDY CREEK and the distinctive Sandy Creek logo
are registered trademarks of Barnes & Noble, Inc.

Text copyright © Ian Whybrow 2005
Illustrations copyright © Tim Warnes 2005

ISBN 978-1-4351-6512-0

Manufactured in China
Lot #:
1 3 5 7 9 8 6 4 2
01/17

www.sterlingpublishing.com